Dogs

Basset Hounds

by Connie Colwell Miller
Consulting Editor: Gail Saunders-Smith, PhD

Consultant: Jennifer Zablotny, DVM
Member, American Veterinary Medical Association

Capstone *press*

Mankato, Minnesota

Pebble Books are published by Capstone Press,
151 Good Counsel Drive, P.O. Box 669, Mankato, Minnesota 56002.
www.capstonepress.com

1 2 3 4 5 6 12 11 10 09 08 07

Library of Congress Cataloging-in-Publication Data
Miller, Connie Colwell, 1976–
Basset hounds / by Connie Colwell Miller.
    p. cm.—(Pebble Books. Dogs)
    Summary: "Simple text and photographs describe basset hounds"—Provided
by publisher.
    Includes bibliographical references and index.
    ISBN-13: 978-0-7368-6741-2 (hardcover)
    ISBN-10: 0-7368-6741-4 (hardcover)
    1. Basset hound—Juvenile literature. I. Title. II. Series.
SF429.B2M55 2007
636.753'6—dc22   2006026739

Note to Parents and Teachers

The Dogs set supports national science standards related to life
science. This book describes and illustrates basset hounds. The
images support early readers in understanding the text. The
repetition of words and phrases helps early readers learn new
words. This book also introduces early readers to subject-specific
vocabulary words, which are defined in the Glossary section. Early
readers may need assistance to read some words and to use the
Table of Contents, Glossary, Read More, Internet Sites, and Index
sections of the book.

Table of Contents

4

Nosy Hound

Basset hounds have
a strong sense of smell.
They help hunters
by sniffing out rabbits.

Basset hounds are
long dogs with short legs.
Their tails point
straight up.

From Puppy to Adult

Basset hound puppies
are small.
They have long ears,
floppy lips, and sad eyes.

Young bassets will grow
into strong, stubborn dogs.
They need training
while they are small.
Trained pups become adult
dogs that behave well.

Full-grown basset hounds need lots of attention. They will howl loudly if left alone.

Basset Hound Care

Basset hounds need food and water every day. Their short legs cannot hold extra weight. Owners should not let them become overweight.

Basset hounds have loose, wrinkly skin. Owners must keep the skin under the wrinkles clean and dry.

Basset hounds have
long ears that are
as soft as velvet.
Owners should clean
their dogs' ears
once each week.

Basset hounds
make good pets.
Owners will enjoy
these smart dogs
for many years.

Glossary

attention—alert care; paying attention includes playing, talking, or being with someone or something.

behave—to act properly

howl—to make a loud, sad noise

overweight—weighing more than is normal

stubborn—not willing to give in or change

train—to teach an animal how to do something

velvet—soft, thick fabric made from cotton, silk, or other materials

wrinkly—covered with lines or folds

Read More

Meister, Cari. *Basset Hounds.* Dogs. Edina, Minn.: Abdo, 2001.

Stone, Lynn M. *Basset Hounds.* Eye to Eye with Dogs. Vero Beach, Fla.: Rourke, 2005.

Internet Sites

FactHound offers a safe, fun way to find Internet sites related to this book. All of the sites on FactHound have been researched by our staff.

Here's how:

1. Visit *www.facthound.com*

2. Choose your grade level.

3. Type in this book ID **0736867414** for age-appropriate sites. You may also browse subjects by clicking on letters, or by clicking on pictures and words.

4. Click on the **Fetch It** button.

FactHound will fetch the best sites for you!

Index

Word Count: 152
Grade: 1
Early-Intervention Level: 14

Editorial Credits
Martha E. H. Rustad, editor; Juliette Peters, set designer; Kyle Grenz, book designer;
    Kara Birr, photo researcher; Scott Thoms, photo editor

Photo Credits
Capstone Press/Karon Dubke, 14, 16, 18
Norvia Behling, 20
Ron Kimball Stock/Ron Kimball, cover, 6
Shutterstock/Chin Kit Sen, 1
UNICORN Stock Photos/Gary Randall, 8
www.jeanmfogle.com, 4, 10, 12